Clifford

The Big Red Dog

The Movie Graphic Novel

Adapted by **Georgia Ball**

Illustrated by **Chi Ngo**

Scholastic Inc.

ISBN 978-1-338-66511-6 (hardcover)

ISBN 978-1-338-66510-9 (paperback)

10 9 8 7 6 21 22 23 24 25

Printed in the U.S.A. 40

First printing 2021 • Edited by Samantha Swank

Art by Chi Ngo • Lettering by Rae Crawford • Book design by Betsy Peterschmidt

New York City.
I thought it was just a stray, but then I saw the puppies . . .

Thanks for calling. These pups will be more comfortable at the shelter.

BANG!

"Chin up!"
WHIMPER...
SCRATCH
Don't be frightened, little fellow.
You're among friends here! Just remember . . .
BRIDWELL'S ANIMAL RESCUE
". . . even scary beginnings can have a bright future."

Harlem.
I know it's important. I wouldn't have asked unless—No, I understand.
I'll figure it out. Okay, thanks.
Emily! How was school?
Somewhere between abysmal and atrocious. So, you know, bad.
I know it's hard being the new kid at school. Are those girls still bothering you?
It's mostly just one girl—Florence. She calls me "Food Stamp" because I'm at school on a scholarship.
You're different from the kids at school. That's good!
People who are unique are the ones who change the world.

Did you talk to your boss about the Chicago thing?
Apparently the trial has been moved up two weeks. I'm the *only* paralegal who . . .
Mom . . .
Sweetheart, if it were up to me, I would never *ever* mi your birthday, but . . .
It's just a few days and then we'll have the best belated birthday dinner ever.
Is Dad still coming to visit?
We've been divorced three years. Has he ever missed your birthday?
I'm sorry Uncle Casey is the only one who could stay with you while I'm gone. I *tried* to find another sitter.
A few days with a guy who thinks green M&MS are a vegetable. Can't wait.
I'm
"Good luck collecting cans for the fund-raiser!"

SNIFF
SNIFF
Get out of here, you little runt!
HONNNNK

Central Park.

Ah, there you are.

Lost, I see. Well, that doesn't make you any less of a treasure.

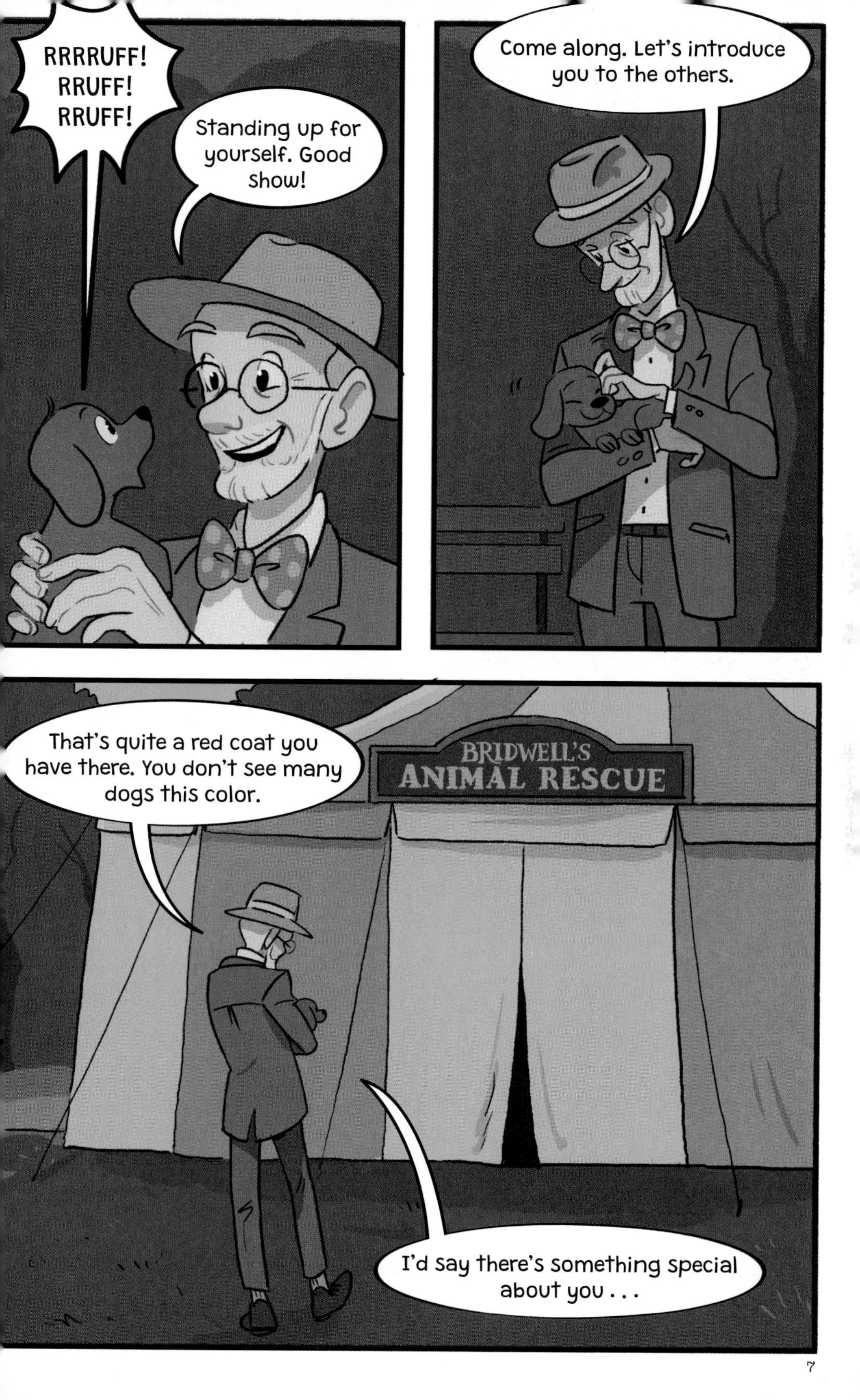
RRRRUFF!
RRUFF!
RRUFF!
Standing up for yourself. Good show!
Come along. Let's introduce you to the others.
That's quite a red coat you have there. You don't see many dogs this color.
BRIDWELL'S ANIMAL RESCUE
I'd say there's something special about you . . .

The next morning, Emily walks with her uncle to school.
I can't believe how many people are awake at this hour. Want to get a coffee?
I'm twelve, Uncle Casey. I can't drink coffee.
Red Bull?
We're going to do something super cool for your birthday. Anything you want. Money's no object—
—as long as your mom left enough of it in the kitchen drawer.
You don't have to worry about my birthday.
I looked on my mom's Facebook account. My dad's planning a surprise for me this weekend.
Wow. He's really pulling out all the stops.
He was asking people for ideas of fun things to do with kids.
That doesn't sound like him at all . . .

BRIDWELL'S ANIMAL RESCUE
Look! An animal rescue . . .
Can we go in? Please?
My instinct is "sure"—so we probably shouldn't.
Ugh, I can't say no to that face!
BRIDWELL'S ANIMAL RESCUE
Plus, they might have free coffee.

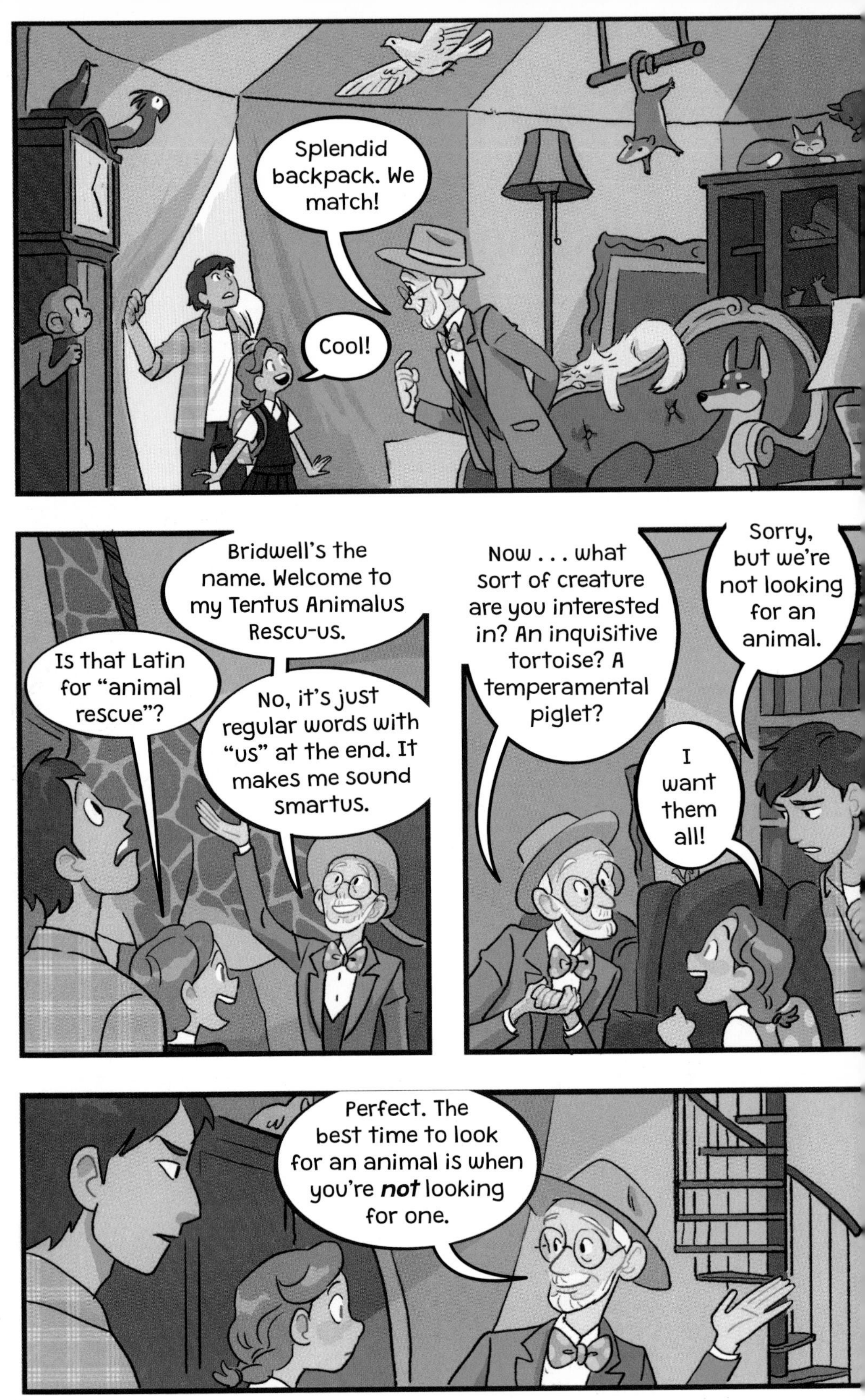
Splendid backpack. We match!
Cool!
Bridwell's the name. Welcome to my Tentus Animalus Rescu-us.
Is that Latin for "animal rescue"?
No, it's just regular words with "us" at the end. It makes me sound smartus.
Now . . . what sort of creature are you interested in? An inquisitive tortoise? A temperamental piglet?
Sorry, but we're not looking for an animal.
I want them all!
Perfect. The best time to look for an animal is when you're *not* looking for one.

OH MY GOSH!
He's so tiny. How big will he get?
That depends, doesn't it?
On what?
Why, on how much you love him, of course!
I think he may have lost his family.
Oh no! I'll be your family, little guy.
Okay. Adorable. Now put him back.
Please, Uncle Casey?
Sorry, but there's no way. I'm supposed to be Responsible Casey now, remember?
And letting you get a micro-dog is *not* responsible.

Thank you for giving me the opportunity to crush my niece's dreams.
I've always wanted to know what it feels like to be the bad guy.
Come on, Emily . . .
You're going to be late for school.
WHIMPER...

OMG, did you bring your ***garbage*** to school?
The cans are for the school recycling fund-raiser. Isn't that today?
Yeah, but nobody actually ***does*** it. Our parents just write the school a check.
HAHAHAHAHAHAHAH
Classic Food Stamp.
. . .

Don't listen to Florence. She's just cranky 'cuz a house fell on her wicked sister.
I think it's awesome that you actually did the work. Really makes you stand out around here.
Pretty much the last thing I was hoping to do— but thanks, Owen.
If it makes you feel any better, I collected cans, too.
Really? Where are they?
My dad forgot what they were and threw them away.
Emily! Owen! Class is starting.

SNICKER
RRRRRRRRIP

HAHAHAHAHAHAHAHAHAHA
Cleanup on aisle four!
CLATTER
CLATTER
CLATTER

Another school day is finally over.
SNIFF

Hey, Em.
How was your—
"Today we're speaking with LyfeGrow CEO, Zac Tieran . . ."
SLAM
That good, huh?
BOOP—BOOP—E—DOOP
DAD
Hello, Emily!
Dad!
Can't wait to see you on Monday.

Monday? But I thought you were coming sooner?
Oh, uh, well . . . I'm, uh . . . not sure what the plan is, but . . . definitely see you on Monday. Right?
Love you, sweetheart. See you soon!
Okay. Bye, Dad.
B
What the . . . ?
RUSTLE
RUSTLE

How did you get in there?
Actually, who cares how. You're the cutest thing I've ever seen!
I better name you. I mean, that's what you do when you get a dog, right?
How about something cool and old-fashioned like . . . Clifford?
RRRUFF!
Can you fetch?
Oh no!

MAYO
Huh?
You?!
I said "no" to the dog and you completely ignored me.
I didn't ignore you—he just showed up. Can't he stay for one night?
Absolutely not! I promised your mom I'd be responsible.

Fine. One night.
But first thing in the morning we're taking him back to the weird old guy in the animal tent!
SOB
SOB
"One night."
I wish we were big and strong so the world couldn't hurt us.

CLICK
♫

The next morning . . .
Oh . . . my . . .

GRRR
No, Clifford!
GRRRRR
POOOOF
Huh . . . This should be interesting.

Good boy, Clifford.
Stop, Clifford!
Sit! Sit!
I guess we need to talk to Uncle Casey.

After a brief freak-out . . .
I'm totally taking Emily to school, Maggie. We're walking to the subway now.
That noise? A bus hit a bookshelf.
Talk later, bye!
I thought you'd be better in a crisis.
We have to find that Bridwell guy and get rid of this dog.
KNOCK KNOCK

It's Packard. I'm here to fix the dishwasher!
It's the building super!
Um . . . One second!
What the heck happened in here?
We couldn't decide what to read?
Literature is tricky.
Where are you going?! The dishwasher's in the kitchen.
The water shutoff valve is in the bedroom closet.
Don't go in there!

There's a lot of girl stuff in there I wouldn't want you to see!
Girls, right? I'll take care of it.
No, Clifford! Stop, stop!
WHACK
WHACK

WHACK
WHACK
WHACK
WHACK
Must be those old pipes, right?

After their close call with Packard, Casey and Emily take Clifford outside.
How is there no info on this Bridwell guy?
You can't just give people pets that go nuclear and ***not*** be on the Internet. It's completely irresponsible.
f we can't nd Bridwell ow are we going to eturn him?
Return him? No. He needs to see a vet.
A vet?
Yeah! What if he's really sick? There's a vet in that big pet store downtown.
CLICK
Fine. We'll bring him to a vet.
But after that, we're finding Bridwell and returning his . . . giant dog . . . thing.

Shouldn't we try to find a way to hide Clifford or something?
He's just a big dog walking down the street. It's New York. People probably won't even notice.
Anyway, we're almost to my truck.
Do you live in here?
Haven't you ever seen a mobile home before?
Not like that.
Look, this is a valid, financially responsible life choice that your mother does not need to know about, okay?

Emily!
Owen?
I thought you were sick, so I skipped P.E. to bring you your homework—
—which I'm suddenly realizing is a lot more awkward than I anticipated.
Ew! What—
AAAAAAAAH
Dogzilla! *Run!*
I guess he's coming along.

LyfeGrow, Inc.
Unfortunately, Mr. Tieran, we're not seeing the kind of genetically induced growth that we were hoping for . . .
We've spent more than $400 million to feed the world more efficiently through genetic engineering. So much money. So much hard work.
I'm sure you must
show for
Well, sir, so far . . .
A two-headed goat. We're trying to feed the world, and you've created more mouths to feed?
I guess you could look at it that way, sir.
I am, and he's looking back at me with four eyes.
I'm not going to lie—it's unsettling. On so many levels.

There's a mold-resistant tomato . . .
Also hammer resistant.
CLANG!
You need to see this. It's all over the Internet.
There's a ten-foot-tall dog in upper Manhattan.

Zac!
Ah, Colette. More good news?

Later that day . . .
Is he all right?
I—I really . . .
Is that a medical opinion? Sounded very scientific.
Well, his teeth are certainly . . . large. That's good.
Should we weigh him?
Of course we should weigh him. We always weigh the animals.
That's part of every exam.

I'll get his temperature . . .
SNIFF
SNIFF
Down, boy!
I think he smells your dog biscuits.
He seems perfectly normal.
Other than being big and red, this dog is healthy as, well, a horse.

That's one big handsome fella you got there.
Thank you very much, Lucille.
I meant the dog. Doc says no charge under the circumstances.
You didn't happen to get him from Bridwell, did you?
How did you know?
I've been working in this office for more than twenty years. Whenever someone brings in a "unique" animal, it always seems to come from him.
Do you think Bridwell could make Clifford small again??
Are you kidding? That's nothing for a man like Bridwell.
Bridwell was at our school yesterday. He would have filled out paperwork with his info.
We have to get to the school.
Do you guys have anything that make giant Elmo here any less . . . noticeable?

I'm not sure this makes him any less noticeable.
This dog's killing me.
Clifford, ***no!*** No fetch! No fetch!

Oh no!
Help!
POP!
HISSSSSSSS
OOOF
Uhhh...
No, Clifford!
Put it down!

Tell me you got that!
That was awesome!
That dog is *huge!*
CLICK
CLICK
CLICK
You *have* to see this . . .
"A miracle . . ."

LyfeGrow, Inc.
Sometimes you pray for a miracle to save your company from ruin, and then . . .
You actually get one.
We don't have anything yet.
We will. It's hard to hide a ten-foot-tall red dog.
When we *do* find it, we want to be sure everyone understands the mutt belongs to us.
This girl appears with the dog in 67% of the images we've examined.
We traced the crest on her uniform to an elite private schoo and found her name—

"—Emily Elizabeth Howard."
Does this truck have Spotify?
What do you think?
We need to get Big Red back there sorted out before your dad's big surprise tomorrow.
Right . . .
Tomorrow.

I'll talk to Clifford.
All right. We get the info on Bridwell and bounce. Cool?
I think he wants good-bye hugs . . .
Stay in the car. We'll be right back.
You'll be okay, big guy.

After Casey distracts the school administrator, Owen goes to work.
I'll lift the intel. Stealth mode. They'll never even know we were here.
That would have sounded a lot cooler if you weren't holding a rainbow flash drive. Where's Em?
"She went to get Clifford a snack."
Hey! Food Stamp! If you're hungry we could organize a food drive—
I'm kind of in a rush—
SQUIRRT
Florence!
I'm so sorry, it was an accident!

You're an accident!
You shouldn't even **be** here. Why do you get to come for free when everyone else has to pay?!
That's the dog that's all over Instagram!

Can we pet him?
Umm . . . sure.
How is he so huge?

Perfect. The biggest nobody in school has the biggest dog in the world. I guess freaks of a feather flock together.
Clifford's not a freak! He's just big.
What did you say to me?
You're just mad because he stole all the attention from you.
HAHAHAHAHAHAHAHAHAHA
And now ***you're*** the same color as Clifford.

Back at Emily's apartment . . .
Standing up to Florence felt really good.
The Wicked Witch is dead!
Focus! After we download the info on Bridwell we need to—
EVICTION NOTICE
I knew I smelled DOG!
Wait— Packard . . . is evicting us?!
This can't be happening . . .
Someone must have sent Packard those pictures of Clifford.
What am I going to say the next time your mother calls?

Did you review the legal disclaimer on self-installation, Mr. Jarvis?
Certainly, Mrs. Jarvis. In what world would I ever—
Whoops!
Help!
I can't hold on . . .
He's slipping!
Somebody help him!
DELI

!?
What the heck . . . ?
It's the giant dog on the news!
I thought I'd lost you, Mr. Jarvis.
Next time we're hirin a handyma Mrs. Jarvi

That dog is amazing!
He saved my life!
Greatest Frisbee catcher on the planet.
Clifford! You're a hero!
Great. He's saving lives and I'm destroying them.
So Packard's okay with you having a pet?
Not exactly. He just evicted us.

You must be Emily Elizabeth.
Who are you?
I'm Zac Tieran from LyfeGrow. Thank you for finding our dog.
A clumsy janitor neglected to secure the gate and our large friend here slipped away from the lab.
I'd like to offer you something for all the inconvenience this must have caused.
I'm really coming around to this guy!
GRRR...
You're lying!
You said Clifford was big when he escaped, but he was small when I first saw him in Bridwell's tent.

Everything okay, Emily?
Everything's fine.
I was asking her.
Alonso!
My arm! Easy! Easy!
I tried to be nice.
HOOWWOOOOOWOOOO
Clifford, **run!**

DELI
Go through our deli—this way!
Don't let them get away!
CRASH

Get Clifford in the truck. I'll be right there!
WHACK
Who are these guys?!
I don't know, Raul . . .
But they're not getting in this deli.

We need to get Clifford out of here!
Do you know how to drive?!
If Uncle Casey can do it, how hard can it be?
VROOOMM
Her mother is literally going to kill me. Metaphorically.
But then also literally.

They're coming!
Head for that building!
Turn! Turn! Turn!

That evening . . .
Thank you for calling to tell me where you are. What's with the Men in Black chasing us?
And where are we?
I live here.
Stay friends with this guy.
SIS
Oh, hi Maggie. Is that a dog? Of course not!
That's just your dishwasher. It's making this weird . . . barking noise.
AARF!!
You should probably find a new apartment.
Oh, I just looked at my battery. It's at like 1%. If I lose you just—

Your mother is
oing to find
ut the truth
sooner or later.
Especially after your dad shows up at a padlocked apartment.
LICK
My dad's not coming tomorrow . . .
What about the big surprise weekend?
That wasn't for me. It was for his new family. He's got a girlfriend.
With kids.
Oh, Em. I'm sorry.
Guys, look at this.

. . . a $25,000 reward for information leading to the capture of this dangerous creature . . .
Dangerous?
Look who's there.
We were in the middle of an experimental trial when it escaped.
The creature is a medical mutant, and that mutation could theoretically jump species.
This animal must be captured and returned to my lab as soon as possible, or the consequences could be catastrophic—
— for everyone.
We need to find Bridwell right away!

checked
he flash
drive.
There was a letter from Bridwell asking the school if he could set up a tent on their property.
One of the dates he said he wasn't available is tomorrow because he's going to be at Old Saint Patrick's Church for their Blessing of the Animals.
We can go see Bridwell at the church!
Emily, the police are looking for Clifford. You've been evicted. We're fugitives!
I don't care.
Clifford came to me when I was alone and had no friends. He's the best part of my life.
I'm ***not*** going to abandon him.

The next morning, Emily brings Clifford to Old Saint Patrick's Church.
Ah, the most famous dog in New York is here!
Let him come.

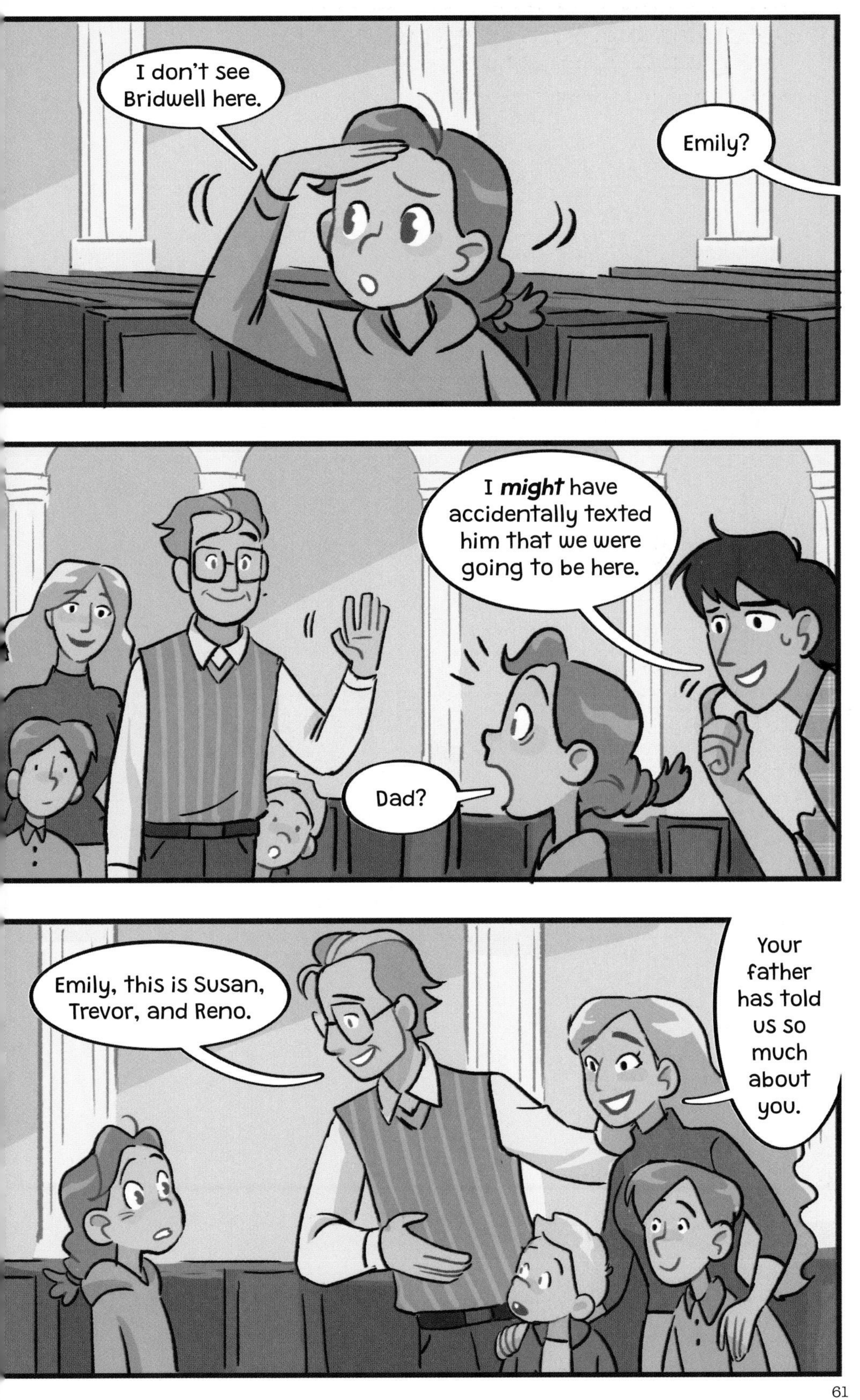
I don't see Bridwell here.
Emily?
I *might* have accidentally texted him that we were going to be here.
Dad?
Emily, this is Susan, Trevor, and Reno.
Your father has told us so much about you.

So, how did you end up with that big guy?
I don't know. How'd you end up with *them?*
Life is complicated, Emily. I should have told you what's been happening in my life. I just didn't want to hurt you.
I know how you must feel . . .
No, you don't. ***Your*** dad didn't leave your family and move to Canada.
You're still my daughter and I love you, Emily.
Happy birthday.
Thanks.
Is everything okay?
Clifford needs me right now. And because I love him—
—I'm not going to let him down.

Is this box from Mr. Bridwell?
Yes. He comes every year, but he's at St. Benedict's Hospital today.
BRIDWELL
He's in room 7203.
I hope Mr. Bridwell is okay . . .
He's the only person who can help us.

St. Benedict's Hospital.
You looking for someone?
Yes. Older man. Tall. Mr. Brid—
Wait. That's his tie! He wears a polka-dot bowtie!
I'm real sorry. The man with that tie . . . your friend . . .
He passed away this morning.
That's impossible . . .
I'm sorry.

He was so nice. He was . . . magical. How could he die?
If there's a memorial, I could email you.
Thank you.
What are we going to do?
EEE-OOO
EEE-OOO
EEE-OO
I bet that's for us. C'mon.

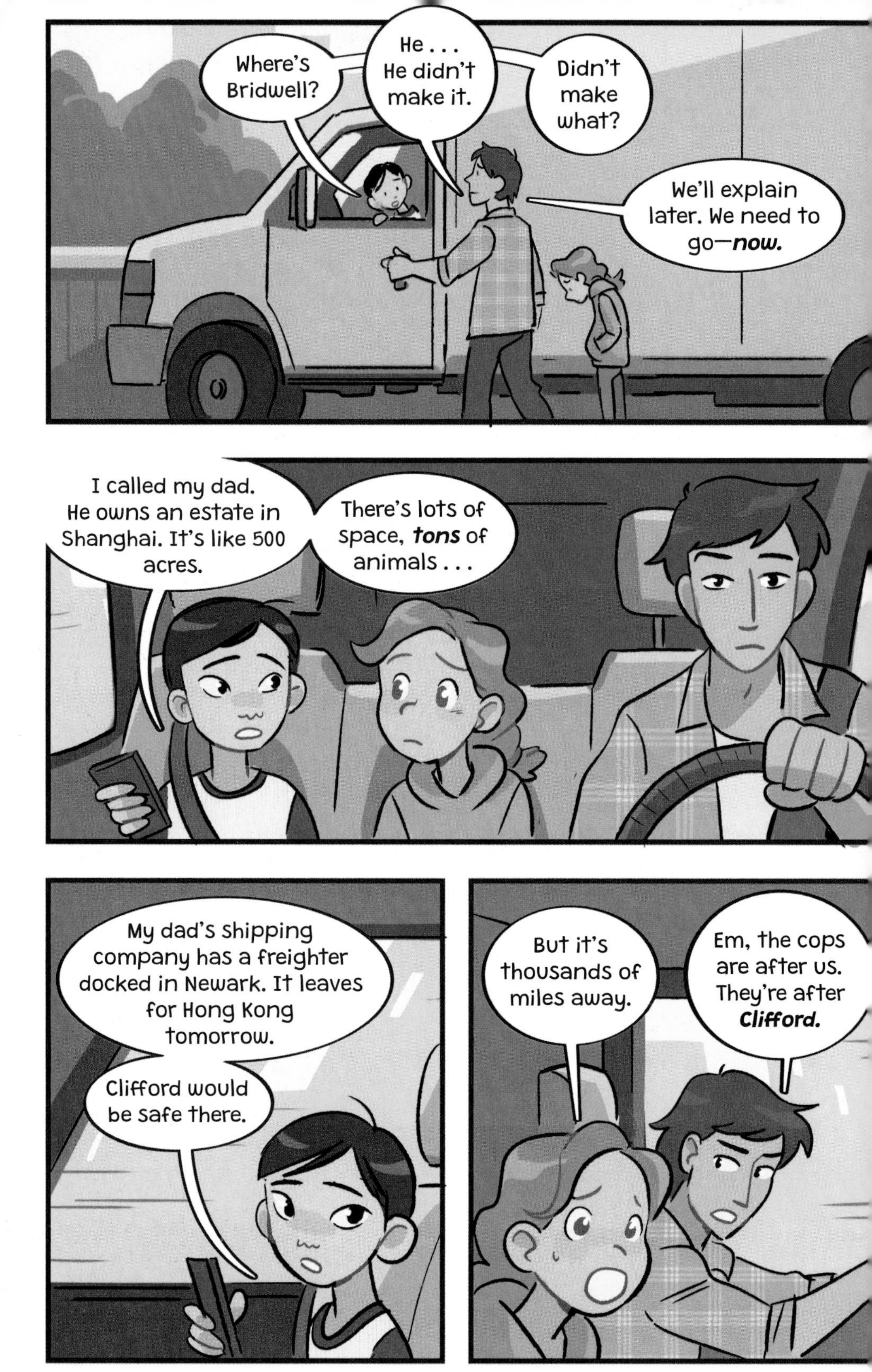
Where's Bridwell?
He . . . He didn't make it.
Didn't make what?
We'll explain later. We need to go—*now.*
I called my dad. He owns an estate in Shanghai. It's like 500 acres.
There's lots of space, *tons* of animals . . .
My dad's shipping company has a freighter docked in Newark. It leaves for Hong Kong tomorrow.
Clifford would be safe there.
But it's thousands of miles away.
Em, the cops are after us. They're after **Clifford.**

Clifford is *not* going to Shanghai without me.
Em . . .
I'm not giving him up!
I'm sorry, Emily. This is not what I wanted either.
I know I said all those things before, but I was wrong.
You and Clifford belong together.
But that's not possible anymore.

You have to do what's best for Clifford.
Not if you can't keep him safe.
But I'm what's best for Clifford.
Sniff...
Okay, Owen.
Call your dad.
We can meet him at the pier tonight.
We should hide out at my apartment until it gets dark.

Later that night . . .
It's all arranged. Colin will stay with Clifford all the way to Shanghai.
When they arrive at port, my staff will bring him to my house.
We can't thank you enough, Mr. Yu.
Thank you.
I'm sorry it worked out like this.
We need to get going.

I let you down. I thought I could save you, but I couldn't.

We have to be big and strong. Remember? So the world can't hurt us.

Emily . . .
You have to go with these men now, Clifford.
Come on, big guy. I got you.
Good-bye, Clifford . . .
"I love you."

Emily and Casey spend the night in the truck.
Aren't you going to eat your muffin?
SIGH
He's going to be happy on that big farm, Em.
My mom's not going to be happy living in the back of a truck.
She called 35 times last night. Do you think she's mad?
Maybe it's time to turn th ringer back on
Huh. That Freddy guy from the hospital sent us the info on Bridwell's memorial.
Wait a second . . .
What?
That's not Bridwell!
Memorial invitation
Freddy must have been talking about a different guy!

Guys! Lucille from the vet's office called—
Bridwell is alive! He's back at Old Saint Patrick's Church.
Emily—look what's on the news!
. . . the tugboat was stopped earlier this morning by the authorities.
LIVE
The dog is being returned to his home at LyfeGrow Labs—the biotech firm that created him as part of their research in genetic engineering . . .

Let's go to our Skycam now to see a live update on this breaking story.
• LIVE
"You're seeing this live—the giant dog has escaped while en route to LyfeGrow Labs!"
"Where *could* the big red dog be going?"
OBJECTS IN THE MIRROR ARE CLOSER THAN THEY APPEAR

Oh my gosh! He's coming home!
You're probably right. We need to make sure we get to him before LyfeGrow does.
LIVE
We're hearing reports that the dog appears to be heading toward midtown!
Then that's where we're going.

We have to hurry!
Yeah, Harlem wants its big red dog back.
I'll talk to her.
Emily? What on earth is going on?
Clifford's in trouble!
Clifford? Who is—
No time to explain.

I'm grounded for life, aren't I?
You and me both.
It's going to take forever to get to midtown.
Floor it, Uncle Casey!
You got this, Em!

HONK
HONK
HONK

There's that big red dog!
Go, Clifford!

We're not letting that dog get away again.

"The police have now joined the chase!"
"Calling all units: He's headed into Manhattan . . ."
Doesn't that girl understand she can't win? This dog is mine.
I think she's kind of cool.

Clifford!
I should've never let you go.

We need to find Mr. Bridwell.
He can help us get Clifford to safety.
Good news—he's right inside!
Got you.

Mr. Bridwell!
Ah, Emily Elizabeth!
Oh my. Somebody's been eating their Wheaties.
We thought you were dead.
Dead? I hope not. I just booked a safari.
I saw your tie at the hospital . . .
Oh, yes. I gave it to a very sick friend of mine who didn't have much time left.
He always loved that tie.

EEE-OOO EEE-OOOO
Mr. Bridwell. You **have** to make Clifford small again or people are going to hurt him.
My dear girl . . .
It was your love that made him big.
"And no one can ever take that away."

EEE-OOO EEE-OOO EEE-OOO EEE-
Emily Elizabeth Howard—for your own safety, step away from the animal. It is dangerous!
Dangerous? He's just a puppy!

That creature is the property of a genetic modification corporation and is a threat to our city.
Clifford is my dog! And he'd never hurt anyone, I swear!
Move in! Watch out, it's violent.
GRRRRR
No, he's scared. Please, leave him alone!
You've got to *do* something, Mr. Bridwell! They're not listening.
They're not? Then why are they here?

Leave him alone!
That dog belongs to the girl!
He hasn't hurt anybody!
The police have the situation under control! Disperse immediately.
You did this?
And you thought you didn't have any friends.
Emily, if you want them to listen, you should speak to them.

My name is Emily Elizabeth, and this is my dog, Clifford.
We love you, Clifford!
Go, Emily!
I know he's bigger and redder than most dogs, but he's also the kindest, most loving dog in the whole wide world.

le looks dangerous to me.
No! He's just different. And I know how he feels because I know what it's like to not fit in, too.

I mean, look at us. Look how different we all are.
"We're from all over the world."
Clifford has brought us all together. He doesn't hate anyone.
He came to me when I was down and alone. And all he did was love me.

Hooray! Bravo! A wonderful speech.
Too bad it doesn't matter.
The animal belongs to LyfeGrow, so if you don't mind . . .
I'd like to claim my property now.

C'mere, dog! Time to come home.

NO LYFEGROW!
NO LYFEGROW!
Sir, do you have any *actual* proof that this dog is yours?
Well . . . no, but—
Then there's nothing we can do.
See? No one can take him away.

The city will send you a bill for our services.
Colette—
I quit.
I love you, Clifford.

Back in Harlem.
Mom!
My bold, brave girl!
Just like you taught me.
I couldn't have done it without my incredibly mature, super responsible uncle.
You have another uncle?
By the way, we got a dog.
I noticed!
You can stay in the apartment as long as you want. And make sure you tell the news ***I'm*** Clifford's best friend!

Three months later . . .
Can Owen come over after school? We need to prep for the Mathalon.
Of course!
KNOCK KNOCK
Clifford
Morning, Em. I hope Clifford is ready for a big day at the park. I've got a brand-new inflatable ball!
Great to see you, Casey!
He's ready to go, but first . . .

He needs his good-bye hug.
See you after school, Clifford—
"—always."
THE END